First published in the United States in 1992 by Chronicle Books. English language translation copyright © 1992 by Chronicle Books. All rights reserved. Originally titled KYORYU NO TANI by Mitsuhiro Kurokawa; supervised by Ikuo Obata. Illustrations and Japanese text copyright© 1991 by Mitsuhiro Kurokawa. English translation rights arranged with KOGUMA Publishing Co., Ltd. through Japan Foreign-Rights Centre. Printed in Singapore.

Kurokawa, Mitsuhiro
    [Kyoryu no tani, chiisana kyoryu oyako no monogatari. [English]
    Dinosaur Valley / by Mitsuhiro Kurokawa
        p. cm.
    Translation of: Kyoryu no tani, chiisana kyoryu oyaku no monogatari.
    Summary: Recreates the behavior and life cycles of several different kinds of dinosaurs. Uses a gate-fold format to present information about prehistoric life and archaeological efforts to reveal the past.
    ISBN 0-8118-0257-4
    1. Dinosaurs—Juvenile literature.   2. Dinosaurs—Pictorial works—Juvenile literature.
3. Toy and moveable books—Specimens.
    [1. Dinosaurs. 2. Toy and moveable books.] I. Title.
    QE862.D5K87 1992
    567.9'1—dc20   92-10788
                                                      CIP
                                                      AC

Cover design by Karen Pike
Type composition by TBH/Typecast, Inc.

Distributed in Canada by Raincoast Books, 112 East Third Avenue, Vancouver, B.C. V5T 1C8

10 9 8 7 6 5 4 3 2 1

Chronicle Books, 275 Fifth Street, San Francisco, California 94103

DINOSAUR VALLEY

Mitsuhiro Kurokawa

Chronicle Books ❀ San Francisco

Seventy million years ago, our planet was very different than it is today. Some places that are now covered by dry and rocky mountains were flooded by warm seas. Humans did not exist, and the earth was roamed by creatures that today live only in our imaginations. This is the story of one such creature.

Orodromeus (Or-oh-dro-me-us) were small plant-eating dinosaurs. They often came to feed along the water's lush shores, which they shared with duck-billed dinosaurs and the many wading birds that lived in the valley.

Like many dinosaurs, this female *Orodromeus* laid her eggs in a sunny, sandy spot in the woods. After she had laid her eggs in a circle, she covered them with plants and leaves to keep the eggs warm and to hide them from animals, like *Struthiomimus* (Strooth-ee-oh-mime-us) and *Ornithomimus* (Or-nith-oh-mime-us), who scratched the valley floor in search of eggs to eat.

The valley was a busy place. Birds swooped across the sky. Bees buzzed from flower to flower. And, occasionally, the air was filled with the thunderous booming of fighting Pachycephalosaurs (Pak-eh-sef-al-oh-soars).

But *Orodromeus* was listening only for the *peep-peep-peep* of her chicks telling her that they were ready to be born.

After a few weeks had passed, she finally heard them. First one peep, then another. Then a rustle and a crack, crack. *Orodromeus* dug the plants off her nest, and then she used her beak to help gently break open the eggs. Inside each shell there was a hatchling small enough to sit in a human's hand.

Even though they were tiny, the baby dinosaurs could walk almost as soon as they poked their heads out of their shells. Because there were so many animals that could eat them, the little dinosaurs had to be able to run away from danger as soon as they were born. *Orodromeus* guided her chicks away from their nest. She walked slowly at first, making sure that none of her babies got lost. All the while, she kept an eye out for the many dangerous predators who lived in the valley.

Orodromeus led the little dinosaurs to a patch of wild strawberries. Just as
they began to nibble the sweet fruit, a pair of *Ornithomimus* raced by.
Orodromeus got her chicks ready to run, but the ostrichlike dinosaurs went
by so quickly, they didn't even notice the little dinosaurs.

15

16

But, as the forest filled with evening mist, the dinosaurs heard the sounds of yet another danger. *Tyrannosaurus* (Tie-ran-oh-soar-us) *rex*, the most ferocious dinosaur in the valley, roared through the trees. *Orodromeus* and her babies hid in the darkness, and the tyrannosaur walked right by.

In the morning, *Orodromeus* took her babies to a river to gather some water plants for breakfast. Many birds, as well as a herd of *Styracosaurus* (Sty-rak-oh-soar-rus), were eating their breakfast, too.

Later, the *Orodromeus* saw a great herd of chasmosaurs (kaz-mo-soars) stampeding through the valley. The youngest chasmosaurs were sheltered in the middle of the pack and the bold, shield-shaped head frills of the adults stood straight up in the air, warning other dinosaurs to stay out of their way. *Orodromeus* and her chicks watched the thundering herd from a distance.

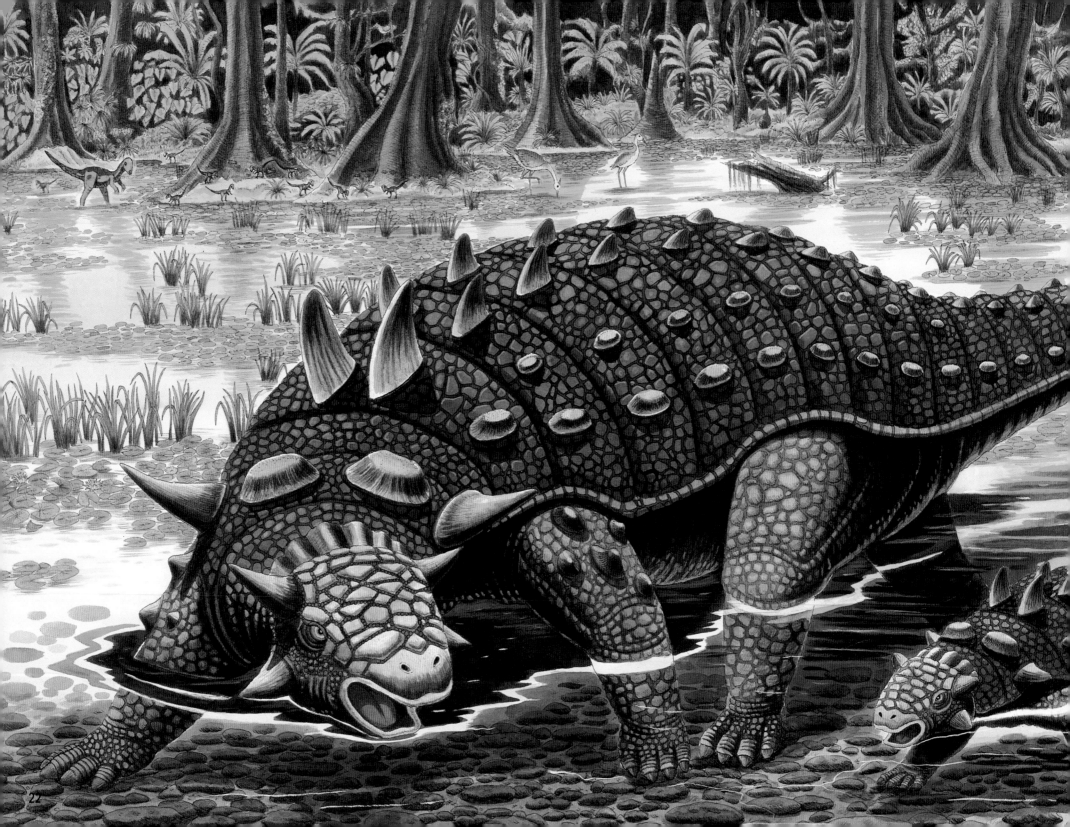

The *Orodromeus* also saw a *Euoplocephalus* (U-oh-ploh-sef-al-us) and her baby. Unlike the chasmosaurs, the euoplocephalosaurs traveled through the valley quietly and alone. Although their spiky armored coats looked frightening, *Orodromeus* knew that these were friendly dinosaurs. But chasing them was a fearsome *Albertosaurus* (Al-bert-oh-saw-rus), a ferocious meat-eater. *Orodromeus* quietly led her babies away from the stream.

Not far away, a fierce battle was raging. This time *Tyrannosaurus rex* had found a lone *Triceratops*. (Tri-ser-a-tops). The tyrannosaur circled round and round trying to attack, but the *Triceratops* brandished its sharp horn and bravely stood its ground. The roars of the giant beasts could be heard across the entire valley. Again, *Orodromeus* quickly guided her babies into the safety of the trees.

Even though her chicks were growing quickly, *Orodromeus* always kept her eye out for danger. This night, however, there was just a pack of peaceful *Parasaurolophus* (Par-a-soar-oh-loaf-us) heading back to their nests.

But danger was never far away. *Orodromeus* could see the eyes of some *Troodon* (True-don) glowing eerily in the twilight. These sharp-clawed dinosaurs were probably her greatest enemy. *Orodromeus* stiffened and hovered protectively over her children, but again they were hidden by the night and the *Troodon* passed them by.

As the chicks grew, *Orodromeus* taught them all her survival skills. She showed them where to find food and where to sleep safely. She taught them which dinosaurs were friendly and how to flee from those who weren't. When they were old enough, the young dinosaurs left their mother to go off into the valley on their own.

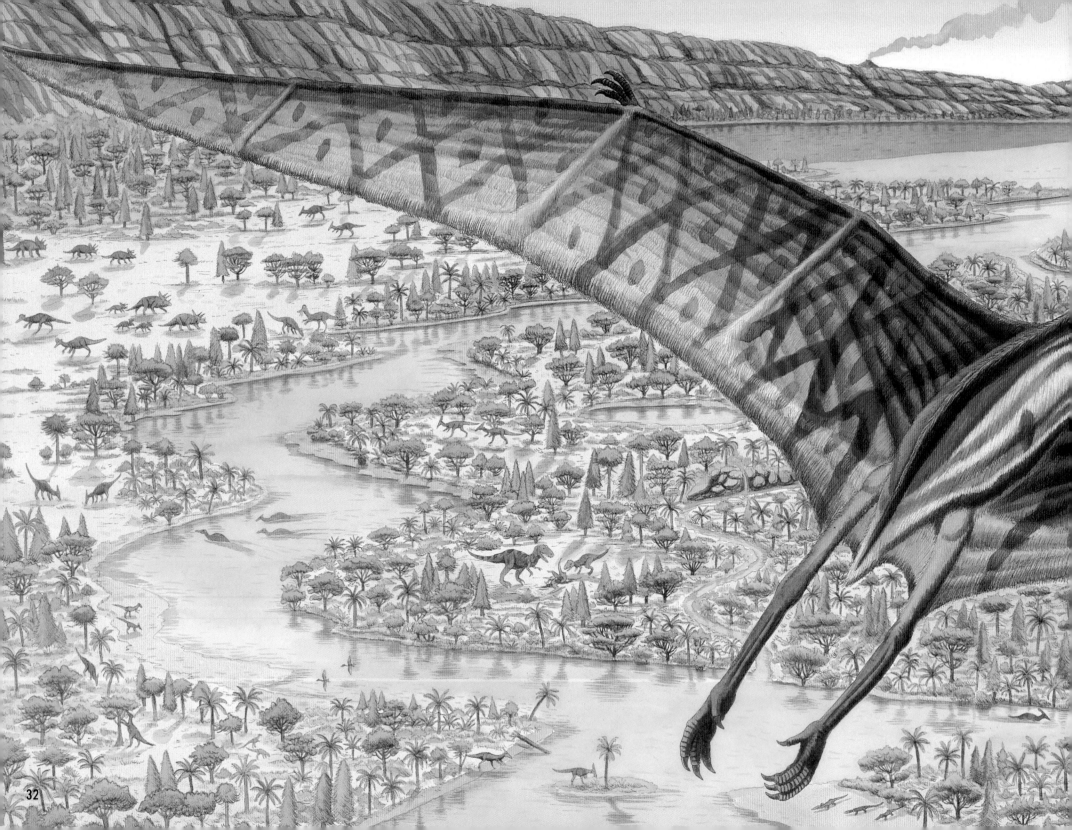

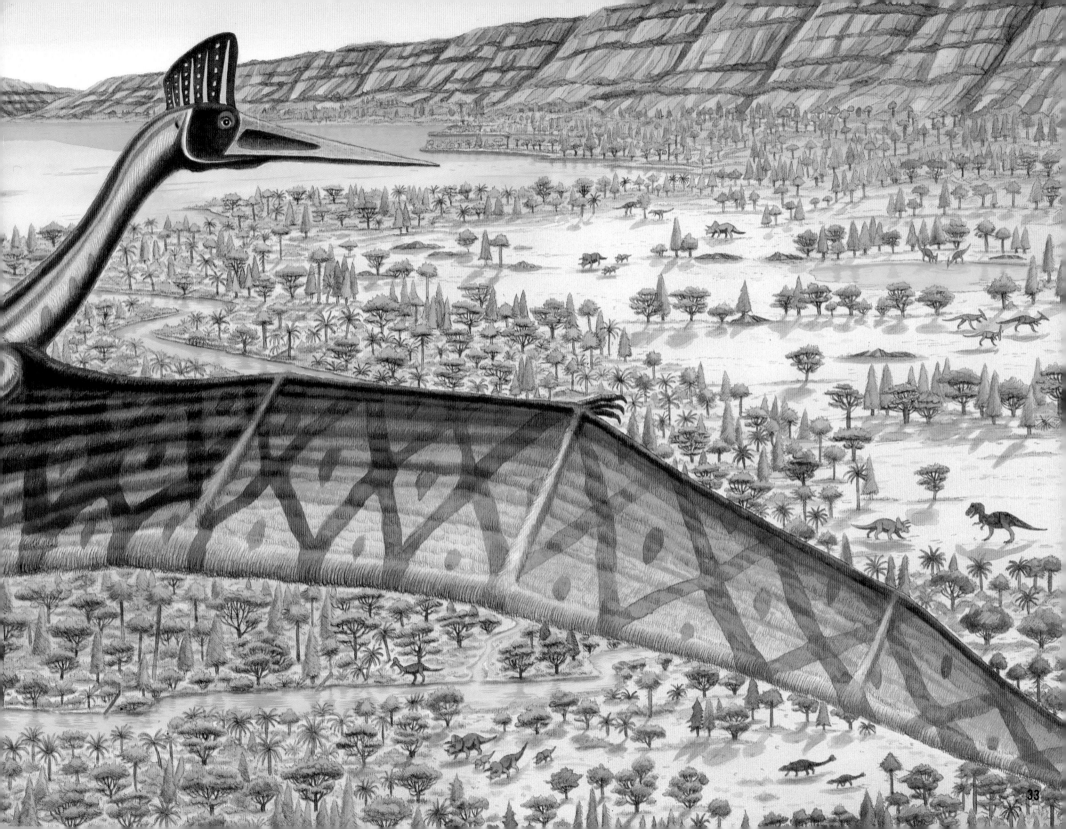

For millions of years, the *Orodromeus* and other dinosaurs ruled the earth. But today all these magnificent animals are gone. Although there are many reasons why they may have disappeared, no one really knows the answer. The scientists who study dinosaurs are called paleontologists. If you lift this page, you can see how these scientists piece together clues about the mysterious creatures who lived and died millions of years ago. Maybe you will find some clues of your own.

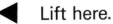 Lift here.

For millions of years, the *Orodromeus* and other dinosaurs ruled the earth. But today all these magnificent animals are gone. Although there are many reasons why they may have disappeared, no one really knows the answer. The scientists who study dinosaurs are called paleontologists. If you lift this page, you can see how these scientists piece together clues about the mysterious creatures who lived and died millions of years ago. Maybe you will find some clues of your own.

◀ Lift here.

18. Tanks of compressed air. 19. Air blower.
20. Fossils are carefully stored while awaiting transport.

21. Small bones are pieced together.
22. Fossilized eggs are excavated.

23. A flatbed truck is used to transport heavy rocks that contain fossils.

24. Cranes are used to lift heavy fossils.

39

11. Plaster jackets are made to protect fossils.
12. Compressed air equipment is also used to blow dirt away from fossils.
13. The excavated fossils are put in order and carefully numbered.
14. Drawings, notes and photographs
15. Motorcycles are sometimes used when looking for bones. They will not damage fossils still underground.
16. Helicopters are often used in case of emergency.
17. Hardhats are worn for protection.

Dino Facts for Older Readers

Some places that are now dry and rocky were covered by seas.

1. *Corythosaurus* (a species of duck-billed dinosaur)
2. A prehisoric bird
3. An *Orodromeus*

The North American continent during the Cretaceous period.

The Red Deer River badlands region in western Canada

❶ An inland sea created a climate quite different from the climate found in the same region today.

The pictures in this story are based on the Red Deer River badlands region in western Canada, but many of the dinosaurs featured were also found in other areas of western North America, such as Montana. During the Cretaceous period these regions were on the shore of an inland sea. Due to the sea's warm currents, the climate was much warmer than

it is today and the region had many wetlands, forests and lakes—much like the environment that now exists along the Gulf of Mexico.
Scientists believe that dinosaurs first appeared during the Triassic period, 220 million years ago. But the dinosaurs that we are most familiar with lived during the Jurassic period (205 to 130 million years

ago) and the Cretaceous period (140 to 65 million years ago). The Cretaceous period is known as the "golden age" of dinosaurs.

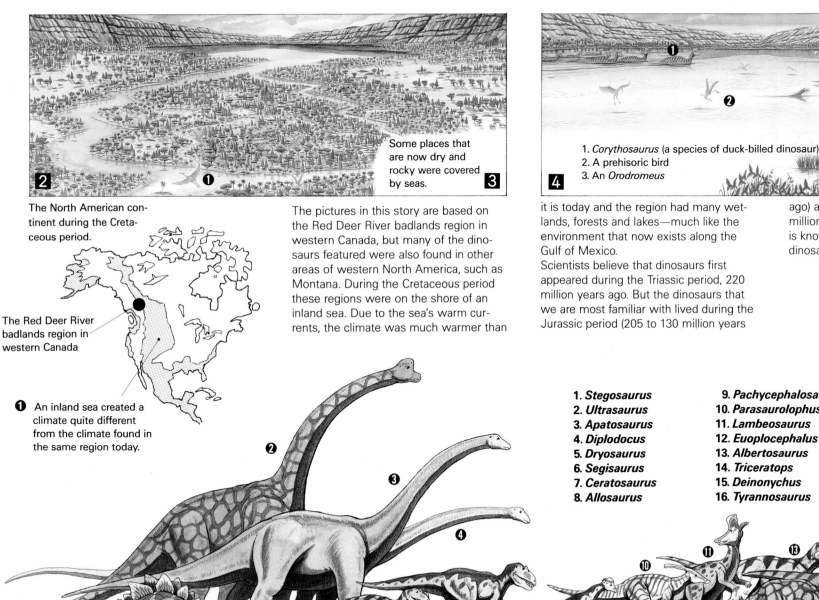

1. **Stegosaurus**
2. **Ultrasaurus**
3. **Apatosaurus**
4. **Diplodocus**
5. **Dryosaurus**
6. **Segisaurus**
7. **Ceratosaurus**
8. **Allosaurus**
9. **Pachycephalosaurus**
10. **Parasaurolophus**
11. **Lambeosaurus**
12. **Euoplocephalus**
13. **Albertosaurus**
14. **Triceratops**
15. **Deinonychus**
16. **Tyrannosaurus**
17. **Orodromeus**
18. **Struthiomimus**
19. **Troodon**

Some of the dinosaurs that lived during the Jurassic period

Some of the dinosaurs that lived during the Cretaceous period

The dinosaur in this story is an Orodromeus of the hypsilophodontid family. Once a hypsilophodontid laid her "clutch", or nest, of eggs, she left them alone. Dinosaurs were simply too big to sit on their eggs.

Hypsilophodontids laid their eggs in a spiral pattern.

Dinosaur chicks probably took several weeks to hatch from their eggs, and their hatching seems to have been more similar to that of birds than to lizards or turtles. As soon as a bird breaks out of its egg, it forms a bond with the first creature it sees, usually its mother. This is known as "imprinting," and it is thought that dinosaur chicks imprinted with their mothers.

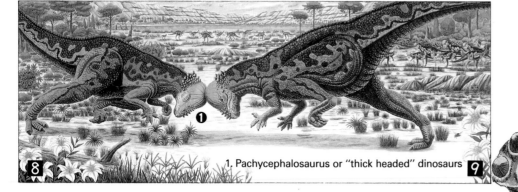

1. Pachycephalosaurus or "thick headed" dinosaurs

Pachycephalosaurus were 15 to 20 feet long and had dome-shaped heads. They were generally peaceful but are believed to have used their heads in butting contests like goats and sheep do today. During the mating season, the males of the group probably rammed heads with each other to determine who would be leader.

The skull of a *Pachycephalosaurus*

A hypsilophodontid egg just before hatching

A chicken egg

The helmetlike skull was 12 inches thick, but its brain was no larger than a doughnut hole

The bumps and spikes along the skull were likely used to attract mates just as today's birds use bright colors

Large eye sockets suggest they had good eyesight

Small teeth that were good for eating plants

Human skull

1. Tyrannosaurus
rex

Hypsilophodontids lived their daily lives in groups, but in order to study them more closely, the mother dinosaur and chicks in this story have been separated from their group. Because they were such easy prey, hypsilophodontid parents needed to protect their young. One way to do this was to flee before they were seen by predators. Another strategy was to hide in clumps of grass. After hiding her chicks, the mother would act as a decoy, leading the attacker far away from the chicks.

Tyrannosaurus rex means "tyrant lizard" and tyrannosaurs are usually thought of as a cruel animals. But, in fact, this large carnivorous dinosaur was essential for maintaining the balance of nature. They kept the dinosaur population at a healthy level and prevented the plant-eating animals from over-grazing and destroying forest habitats. Tyrannosaurs also ate dinosaurs that were already dead, helping to keep the forest and lakes clean.

1./2. One common predator of hypsilo-phodontid eggs were the ornitho-mimids, which means "bird mimic."

Ornithomimids, or Ostrich dinosaurs, had bodies perfectly designed for running. They were probably the fastest of all dinosaurs and may have been faster than the modern-day ostrich. Scientists think they ate fruits, insects and the eggs of other dinosaurs.

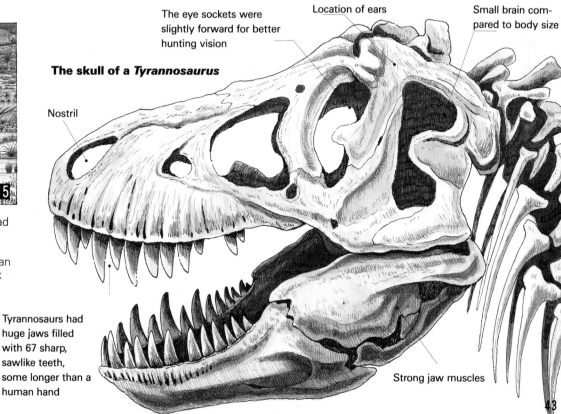

The eye sockets were slightly forward for better hunting vision

Location of ears

Small brain compared to body size

The skull of a *Tyrannosaurus*

Nostril

Tyrannosaurs had huge jaws filled with 67 sharp, sawlike teeth, some longer than a human hand

Strong jaw muscles

1. *Styracosaurus*

18 19

22 23

1. *Euoplocephalus*
2. A large meat-eating
Albertosaurus

Styracosaurus means "spiked reptile." Its skull had six long spikes.

Like modern-day animals, dinosaurs frequently gathered at springs to drink water and to cool off. Here they met many other different kinds of dinosaurs, but they also had to keep a careful eye out for predators that would also come to these areas in search of prey.

Euoplocephalus was a member of the Ankylosauria family. Ankylosauria means "armored bodies." Euoplocephalus were herbivores with a hard, thick shell that protected their bodies. They had a heavy bone-like lump on their tales which could be used as a weapon against predators.

Even their eyelids were made of bone.

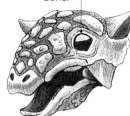

Skeleton of mantle

These openings kept the large skull from being too heavy

***Chasmosaurus* skeleton**

A strong backbone was needed to support the heavy head-frill

1. *Chasmosaurus*, or "cleft lizard"

20 21

Like some birds and reptiles today, dinosaurs probably displayed a wealth of colors and patterns. The large mantle or head-frill of the chasmosaurs may have been used to frighten predators or to attract mates.

Thick, strong legs

44

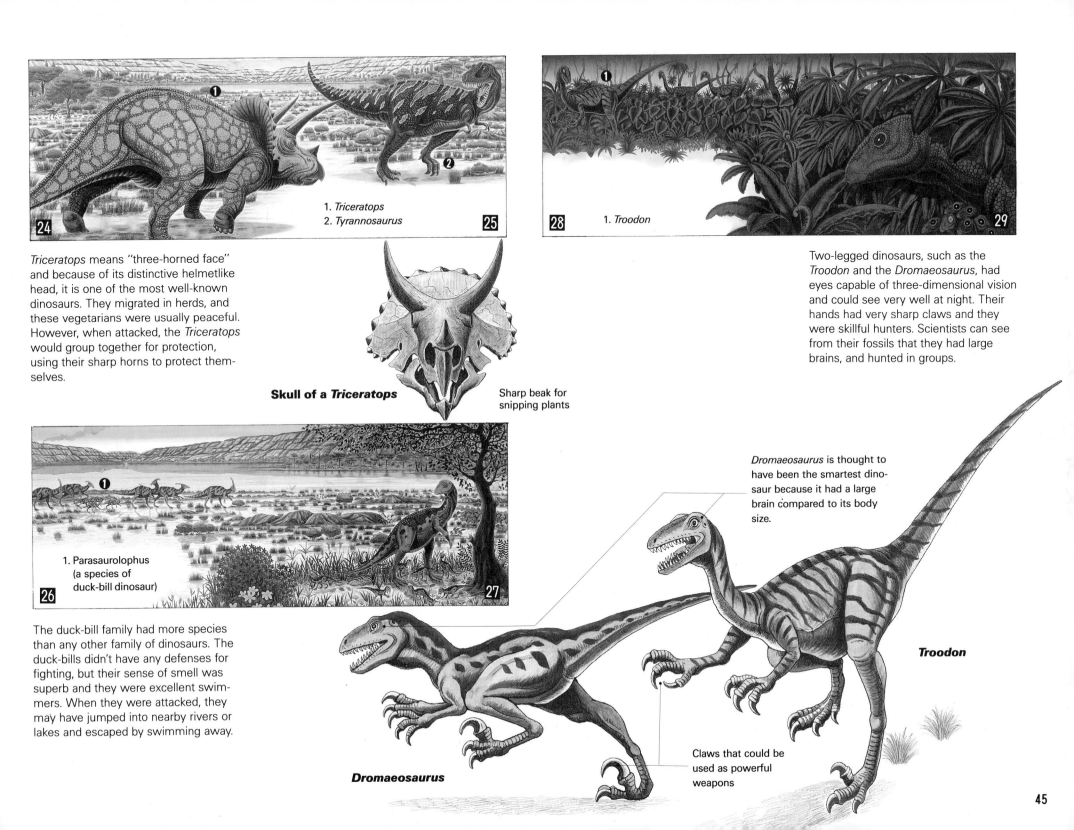

1. *Triceratops*
2. *Tyrannosaurus*

Skull of a *Triceratops*

Sharp beak for snipping plants

1. Parasaurolophus (a species of duck-bill dinosaur)

1. *Troodon*

Triceratops means "three-horned face" and because of its distinctive helmetlike head, it is one of the most well-known dinosaurs. They migrated in herds, and these vegetarians were usually peaceful. However, when attacked, the *Triceratops* would group together for protection, using their sharp horns to protect themselves.

The duck-bill family had more species than any other family of dinosaurs. The duck-bills didn't have any defenses for fighting, but their sense of smell was superb and they were excellent swimmers. When they were attacked, they may have jumped into nearby rivers or lakes and escaped by swimming away.

Two-legged dinosaurs, such as the *Troodon* and the *Dromaeosaurus*, had eyes capable of three-dimensional vision and could see very well at night. Their hands had very sharp claws and they were skillful hunters. Scientists can see from their fossils that they had large brains, and hunted in groups.

Dromaeosaurus is thought to have been the smartest dinosaur because it had a large brain compared to its body size.

Claws that could be used as powerful weapons

Dromaeosaurus

Troodon

1. Small mammals also appeared during this period.

30 31

Hypsilophodontids were often the prey of meat-eaters. Nonetheless, they prospered for 70 million years, from the late Jurassic period to the end of the Cretaceous period.

1. The Skull of a *Triceratops* could be as wide as 7 feet and weigh as much as 1,000 pounds
2. Mammals

34 35

A variety of theories have tried to explain why dinosaurs disappeared . Some people think that a huge meteor smashed into the earth and caused a drastic change in climate. Others believe erupting volcanoes may have caused the change in climate and the extinction of numerous species. But no one knows truly the reason for their disappearance. It is one of science's greatest mysteries.

Gliding or flying prehistoric reptiles are called Pterosaurs. These were not the same as dinosaurs. No dinosaurs were capable of flying.

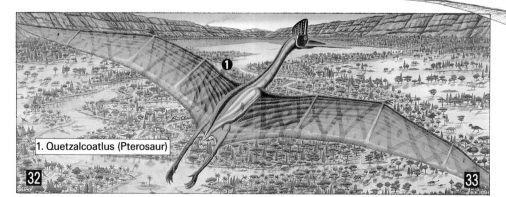

1. Quetzalcoatlus (Pterosaur)

32 33

Long ago, native South and Central Americans of the Aztec civilization worshipped a "winged snake" they called Quetzalcoatl. When the large, winged pterosaur, shown here, was discovered by scientists, they named it after the Aztec god. It is the largest flying animal ever to have lived.

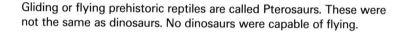

Dsungaripterus (Cretaceous)

Pteranodon (Cretaceous)

Quetzalcoatlus (Cretaceous)

Dimorphodon (Jurassic)

Rhamphorhynchus (Jurassic)

Rhamphorhynchus (Jurassic)

It is rare to find fossils with skeletons in their original form, as in this picture. They are usually scattered over a large area. At an excavation site, museum researchers, preparators, and volunteers work carefully to excavate the broken pieces a little bit at a time. Because fossils begin to deteriorate rapidly when they are exposed to air and sun, they are often covered with plaster or coated with a hardening agent to protect them. Sometimes the fossils are transported to museums or research centers with the dirt and rocks still around them. Helicopters and cranes as well as trucks are used to move fossils.

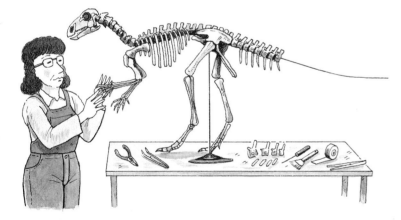

Excavated fossils are transported to a laboratory while still encased in dirt and rocks, and are carefully prepared by an expert. Sometimes it takes several years to assemble a fossil.

A dental drill, among other tools, is used for cleaning and to remove a fossil from rocks.

47

A Note from the Editor

Dinosaur fossils have been around for almost two hundred million years, but it has been only since the middle of the nineteenth century that humans have known what kind of animals they belonged to. In 1841, Sir Richard Owen (the first head of the British Museum) announced that the bones were the remains of extinct prehistoric reptiles, and he coined the word dinosaur from the Greek words *deinos* ("terrible") and *sauros* ("lizard"). Sir Owen's announcment was startling because the theory of extinction was very new.

Fossils are formed when an animal (or plant) dies and becomes buried by mud, water or sand. Over the course of time, the bones (or skin) are changed into hard minerals. After millions of years, the fossils are exposed—by the wind and rain or by a paleontologist's shovel—and discovered by some lucky person. Everything we know about dinosaurs we have learned from fossils.

Fossils can tell us about the size of the animal, its probable diet (tyrannosaurs have teeth that are ridged like steak knives so we believe they ate meat) and about growth. But fossils can't tell us everything about the animals they came from. They can't tell us the color of their skin, the way they lived their day-to-day lives, or the sounds they made. These things we can only guess.

Traditionally, dinosaurs have been portrayed as slow, stupid animals that were dull in color and had little communal life. But recently, scientists have unearthed clues that have led them to believe that many dinosaurs may have been fast-moving, that they were probably as smart as some of their modern bird and reptilian relatives, and that like some of those relatives they may even have been brightly colored. It is also believed that some dinosaurs cared for their young for extended periods of time (more like modern birds than like turtles, for example, whose young are left on their own as soon as they are born).

More than two hundred and fifty dinosaur species have been identified. They come in all shapes and sizes, some bigger than a house, others as small as a chicken. And new species are being unearthed regularly—at a rate of about six per year. This book highlights some of the most famous species. Hopefully it will help you to imagine dinosaurs as living, breathing, noisy animals rather than the quiet, dusty skeletons you see in museums. Maybe it will even inspire you to study dinosaurs. Who knows?—someday there may be a dinosaur named after *you*.

Glossary

carnivorous: meat-eating.

clutch: a group of eggs.

Cretaceous: (Cri-tay-shus) the last period of the Mesozoic era—this period between 140 to 65 million years ago is known as the "golden age" of dinosaurs. During this time dinosaurs peaked and then became extinct.

dig: a site where paleontologists (scientists) search for fossils.

dinosaur: any of a group of extinct prehistoric reptiles. Their closest living relative is the crocodile, though many scientists believe that other reptiles, as well as birds, are their modern descendants.

excavation: the process of removing fossils from a dig site.

extinct: no longer living or in existence.

fossil: the remains of something that was alive.

habitat: the place where a plant or animal lives and grows (includes climate, temperature, amount of oxygen, etc.).

herbivorous: feeding mainly on plants.

herd: a group of one kind of animal that lives and travels together.

Jurassic: (Jur-as-ik) the second geological period of the Mesozoic era—205 to 140 million years ago.

mammal: an animal that is warm-blooded and covered with hair (such as fur, wool, or quills). Mammals give birth to live young and feed their young with milk.

Mesozoic: (Mez-o-zo-ik) this era is known as the Age of Dinosaurs and occurred from 225 to 65 million years ago. The Triassic, Jurassic and Cretaceous periods are the three periods which make up the Mesozoic era.

paleontologist: (pay-lee-on-tol-o-jist) a scientist who studies past life by finding and identifying fossils.

predator: an animal that hunts for and eats other animals.

preparator: someone who prepares scientific specimens, like fossils, for study or display.

prey: an animal that is hunted as food.

reptile: an animal that has scales and whose body temperature is affected by the environment. (Includes lizards, snakes, turtles, crocodiles and alligators.)

skeleton: the bony framework inside a body.

skull: the skeleton of a head; bone structure that protects the brain and supports the jaws.

species: a group of animals or plants that share common physical traits and are able to reproduce with each other.

Triassic: (Try-as-ik) the period of time between 225 and 190 million years ago. It was during this earliest period of the Mesozoic era that dinosaurs first appeared.

Dinosaur names:

Albertosaurus (Al-bert-oh-soar-rus): This 26-foot dinosaur was smaller than a tyrannosaur, but it was also a fierce meat-eater.

Chasmosaurus (Kaz-mo-soar-us): This 17-foot carnivorous dinosaur was one of the first long-frilled ceratopsians ("horned face reptiles"). Since its large frill was hollow, scientists believe it was used to attract mates or to warn away predators rather than for any real protection.

Corythosaurus (Cor-ee-tho-soar-us): means "helmet reptile," and it was so named because the scientist that discovered its fossil thought that it looked like a gladiator's helmet. These 33 foot dinosaurs are one of the best known hadrosaurs, or duckbilled dinosaurs. Each one had up to 2,000 teeth, which were used to grind up plants for food.

Euoplocephalus (U-oh-ploh-sef-a-lus): This 22-foot armored dinosaur weighed a lot, but like the modern rhinocerus, it could probably run fast for short periods of time.

Ornithomimus (Or-nith-oh-mime-us): means "bird mimic," and, like modern birds, it probably chopped food with its beak and swallowed it in chunks. Scientists believe it ate leaves, fruits, insects, lizards and small mammals.

Orodromeus (Or-oh-dro-me-us): a species of dinosaur known as hypsilophodonts. Good at evolving, hypsilophodonts of one kind or another existed for 100 million years.

Pachycephalusaur (Pak-ee-sef-al-oh-soar): means "thick-headed dinosaur." This 15-foot dinosaur was named for its hard skull, which could be up to 12 inches thick.

Parasaurolophus (Par-a-soar-o-lo-fus): was another species of duck-billed dinosaur. Like the corythosaurus, its distinctive crest may have had a horn of some sort that was used to attract mates or simply to allow members of the species to recognize one another.

Pterosaur (Ter-oh-soar): means "winged lizards" and these flying reptiles appeared and disappeared at the same time as the dinosaurs.

Quetzalcoatlus (ket-sal-kwat-lus): is a species of pterosaur. It was named after an Aztec god and it is the largest flying animal that has ever lived.

Struthiomimus (Strooth-ee-oh-mime-us): means "ostrich mimic." This 12-foot dinosaur was very fast and may have used its hands to dig for food.

Styracosaurus (Sty-ra-co-soar-us): means "spiked reptile." This 18-foot dinosaur probably used its six spiny horns to protect itself against predators and to ward off rivals of its own species.

Triceratops (Tri-ser-a-tops): means "three horned face." This 30-foot dinosaur is often called the "last of the dinosaurs" because its fossils have been found in the most recent rock sediments containing dinosaur remains.

Troodon (True-don): was a lightly built dinosaur, about 6 feet long. Quick and agile, this ferocious meat-eater used its large claws to hunt for food.

Tyrannosaurus rex (Ty-ran-oh-soar-us rex): means "tyrant reptile." Perhaps the most famous of all dinosaurs, it is probably the largest meat-eater ever to have lived. As tall as an eight-story building, a human would barely have reached a tyrannosaur's knee.